GOLDEN FAIRY TALE COLLECTION

ILLUSTRATED BY TONY WOLF
TEXT BY PETER HOLEINONE

© DAMI EDITORE, ITALY

Published by Tormont Publications Inc.
338 Saint Antoine St. E.
Montreal, Quebec
CANADA H2Y IA3

Printed in Italy

PRINTED BY
ARTI GRAFICHE MOTTA
MILANO - ITALY

The story of

THE
TIN SOLDIER

and other tales

Once upon a time . . .

. . . there lived a little tin soldier. Even though he had been made just like all other tin soldiers, he had a heart and feelings. Here is the extraordinary story of his adventures.

THE TIN SOLDIER

Once upon a time . . . there lived a child who had a lot of toys. The child kept his toys in his room and spent many happy hours everyday playing with them. One of his favourite games was the battle with the tin soldiers. He arranged the little toy soldiers in their respective ranks and fought imaginary battles.

When the boy received the soldiers, as a present, he noticed that one of them had been made, by mistake, with just one leg. Despite the missing limb, the boy placed the little mutilated soldier in the front lines, encouraging him to be the most valorous of all the little soldiers. The child did not know that, at night, the toys became animated and talked between themselves.

It often happened that, when lining up the soldiers after playing with them, the little boy would forget about the little tin soldier without a leg and left him with all the other toys. It was thus that the little metal soldier got to talk to a pretty tin ballerina.

A great friendship was born between the two, and pretty soon the little soldier fell in love with the ballerina. But the nights went by quickly, and he did not find the courage to declare his love to her. When the child played with the soldiers and positioned him in the front lines, the little soldier hoped that the ballerina would notice his courage in battle. And in the evening, when the ballerina asked the soldier if he had been afraid, he proudly answered, "No."

But the loving stares and sighs of the little soldier did not go unnoticed by the jack-in-the-box. One night, the jack-in-the-box said to the little soldier: "Hey you! Don't look at the ballerina like that!" The poor little soldier was confused and he blushed, but the kind ballerina cheered him up.

"Don't listen to him, he is ugly and jealous. I am very happy to talk to you," she said blushing too. The two little tin figurines were both too shy to speak of their love.

One day they were separated. The boy picked up the tin soldier and placed him on the window-sill.

"You stay here and watch for the enemy," he said. Then the boy played inside with the other soliders.

It was summer and in the days that followed the soldier remained on the window-sill. But one afternoon there was a sudden storm and a strong wind shook the windows. The little soldier fell head first off the window-sill. His bayonet stuck into the ground. It kept raining and storming and pretty soon the rain formed big puddles and the gutters were full. A group of boys in the nearby school waited for the storm to end and when it stopped raining hard they ran outdoors.

Joking and laughing, the boys hopped over the bigger puddles while two of them cautiously walked next to the wall so that the sprinkling rain wouldn't wet them. These two boys noticed the little tin soldier stuck in the sodden earth.

"Too bad he has just one leg. Otherwise, I'd take him home with me," one of the boys said. The other boy picked him up and put him in his pocket.

"Let's take him anyway," he said. "We could use him for something." On the other side of the street, the gutter was overflowing and the current carried a little paper boat.

"Let's put the little soldier in the boat and make him a sailor," said the boy who had picked up the tin soldier. And so the little soldier became a sailor.

The whirling gutter flowed into a sewer and the little
boat was carried down the drain. The water in the
underground sewage was deep and muddy. Big rats
gnashed their teeth as the vessel and its unusual passenger
flowed by. The boat was soaked and about to sink. But the
little soldier, who had faced far greater dangers in battle,
was not afraid. The water of the sewer then flowed into the

river and the little boat, now overturned, was swept by the high waves. The little tin soldier realized his end was near. After the paper boat was wrecked, he sank in deep waters. A thousand thoughts went through the little soldier's mind, but one in particular anguished him:

"I will never see my sweet little ballerina again!" But a huge mouth swallowed the little tin soldier and, once again, his destiny took an unexpected turn.

The little soldier found himself in the stomach of a large fish who had been lured by the glittering colours of his uniform. The fish, however, did not even have time to digest his meal because, shortly after having swallowed the soldier, he was caught in the net of a fisherman. Shortly after, the gasping fish ended up in a big basket and was brought to the market.

Meanwhile, a cook was on her way to the market. She worked in the very same house where the little soldier used to live.

"This fish will be perfect for tonight's guests," the cook said when she saw the big fish on the fish market's counter. The fish ended up in the kitchen and when the cook slit its belly to clean it she found the little tin soldier.

"This looks like one of our boy's toy soldiers . . ." she thought, and ran to the boy to show him her discovery.

"That's right, it's my soldier!" the little boy cheered, when he recognized the soldier with the missing leg.

"I wonder how he got into the fish's belly? Poor soldier, he must have gone through a lot of trouble since he fell off the window-sill!" The little boy placed the soldier on the mantle, right next to his sister's ballerina.

The amazing ways of destiny had once again reunited the two lovers. The little soldier and the ballerina were very happy to be close to each other. At night they talked about what had happened after their separation. But the ill disposition of fate had another surprise in store for them.

One day a sudden gust of wind lifted the heavy drape of the window and hit the ballerina, who fell into the fireplace. The little soldier saw his friend fall into the fireplace and he was frightened. He knew a fire was lit because he could feel its warmth. He was desperate, conscious of not being able to do anything to save the ballerina. In fact, fire is the greatest enemy of tin figurines because it melts metals. Rocking back and forth on his one leg, the little soldier tried to move the metal base under his feet that held him in place.

He kept trying to move until he fell into the fire as well. The two figurines were reunited in their misfortune. They were so close to each other now, that their metal bases began melting together. The tin of one base melted with the metal of the other, and the metal strangely moulded into the shape of a heart. As their bodies were about to begin melting as well, the little boy went by the fireplace and saw the two little figurines enveloped by the flames and moved them away from the blaze with his foot.

Ever since then the soldier and the ballerina have been melted close to each other, sharing their destiny and a common base shaped like a heart.

THE ELVES AND THE SHOEMAKER

Once upon a time there lived a poor shoemaker. He lived in misery because as he grew old he could not see all that well anymore and, consequently he could not work like he used to.

One night he went to bed sad, without finishing a repair job he had begun. In the morning he found the job done.

During the day he set out all the tools and material necessary to make a new pair of shoes for a rich customer.

"Tomorrow morning, when it will be sunny and bright, I will begin working on them," he thought. But the morning after, instead of the leather he had left the night before, the shoemaker was very surprised to find a beautiful pair of brand new shoes. Later on in the day, the customer went by the shop to see how his new shoes were coming along. When he found a very nice pair of shoes ready, he was very happy and paid the shoemaker twice the price they had agreed upon.

The shoemaker was very confused and wondered what had happened. That night, he left out some more leather and the next morning he found another shiny and perfect pair of new

shoes. These shoes were sold at an even higher price. Now the shoemaker left out leather and tools to his mysterious helper every night, and, every morning, he found a new pair of shoes. Pretty soon, the shoemaker was able to save a good sum of money. When the shoemaker's wife noticed all the money the shoemaker had saved, she grew suspicious and demanded an explanation. When she was informed of the unusual nocturnal occurrences, she proposed:

"Let's wait until nightfall. We will hide and find out what's happening."

And so the shoemaker and his wife hid and, around midnight, saw two elves sneak into the shoemaker's shop. The quick and skilled elves made a new pair of shoes in a flash. It was winter and the elves, dressed in ragged clothes, shivered while they worked.

"Poor fellows! They must be very cold," the shoemaker's wife whispered to her husband. "Tomorrow I will make them two heavy wool jackets. That way they will be warmer and maybe, instead of one pair of shoes, they will make two!"

The following midnight, next to the leather, the two elves found two elegant red jackets with gold buttons. They put on the jackets and were very happy. They danced shouting:

"What beautiful jackets! We'll never be cold again." But when one of the elves said:

"Let's get to work now," the other answered:

"Work? What for? With two jackets like these we are rich. We will never have to work again."

The two elves left the shop of the astonished shoemaker and his even more puzzled wife and were never seen again.

THE TAIL OF THE BEAR

Once upon a time there lived a fisherman who earned a living selling fish, making his rounds to the customers on a horse-drawn cart loaded with his catch of the day.

One cold winter day, while the fisherman was crossing the woods, a fox smelled the fish and began following the cart at a close distance. The fisherman kept his trout in long wicker baskets and the sight of the fish made the fox's mouth water. The fox, however, was reluctant to jump on the cart to steal a fish because the fisherman had a long whip that he cracked from time to time to spur on the horse. But the smell of fresh fish was so enticing that the fox overcame her fear of the whip, leapt on to the cart and with a quick blow of her paw, dropped a wicker basket on the snow. The fisherman did not notice anything and continued his journey undisturbed.

The fox was very happy. She opened the basket and got ready to enjoy her meal. She was about to taste the first bite when a bear appeared.

"Where did you get all that marvellous trout?" the big bear asked with a hungry look on its face.

"I've been fishing," the fox answered, unperturbed.

"Fishing? How? The lake is frozen over," the bear said, incredulously. "How did you manage to fish?"

The fox was aware that, unless she could get rid of the bear with some kind of excuse, she would have had to share her fish. But the only plausible answer she could come up with was:

"I fished with my tail."

"With your tail?" said the bear, who was even more astonished.

"Sure, with my tail. I made a hole in the ice, I dropped my tail in the water and when I felt a bite I pulled it out and a fish was stuck on its end," the fox told the bear. The bear touched his tail and his mouth began watering. He said:

"Thanks for the tip. I'm going fishing too."

The lake was not too far away, but the ice was very thick and the bear had a hard time making a hole in it. Finally, his long claws got the job done. As time went by and evening approached, it got colder and colder. The bear shivered but he kept sitting by the hole with his tail in the water. No fish had bitten yet.

The bear was very cold and the water of the lake began freezing again around his tail. It was then that the bear felt something like a bite on the end of his frozen tail. The bear pulled with all his strength, heard something tear and at the same time felt a very sharp pain. He turned around to find out what kind of fish he had caught, and right then he realized that his tail, trapped in the ice, had been torn off.

Ever since then, bears have had a little stump instead of a long and thick tail.

A SHREWD FARMER'S STORY

Once upon a time there lived a farmer who worked far from his home in the fields of a rich baron.

In the past, gangs of bandits hid in the mountains rising behind the plain but the emperor had sent his soldiers to find and kill the thieves and now the area was safe and quiet. Every once in a while, however, old weapons from past battles could be found in the fields.

While he was chopping a stump one day, the farmer found a bag full of gold. The farmer had only ever seen silver coins in his life, and he was so astonished to find all that gold, that when he started walking home it was already dark. On his way home, the farmer thought about the problems that this sudden wealth could cause him.

First of all, everything found on the baron's territory belonged to the baron. By law, the farmer had to hand the gold over to the baron. The farmer decided that it was much more fair for him to keep the treasure because he was very poor, rather than giving it to the baron who already had a lot of money. He realized the risk he would run if anyone found out about his luck. He would never tell anyone, of course, but his wife had a reputation for talking too much and she would never keep a secret. Sooner or later he would end up in jail.

He thought the problem over and over until he found a solution. Before getting home he left the bag full of gold in a bush next to some pine trees and the day after, instead of going to work, he went by the village to buy a few nice trout, some doughnuts and a rabbit. In the afternoon he went home and said to his wife:

"Get your wicker basket and come with me. Yesterday it rained and the wood is full of mushrooms. We must get to them before someone else does!" The wife, who loved mushrooms, picked up her basket and followed her husband. When they got to the woods the farmer ran to his wife shouting:

"Look! Look! We have found a doughnut tree!" and he showed her the branches he had previously loaded with doughnuts.

The wife was astonished but she was even more puzzled when, instead of mushrooms, she found trout in the grass. The farmer laughed happily.

"Today is our lucky day! My grandfather said that everyone has one lucky day. We might even find a treasure!" In addition to being a gossip, the farmer's wife was also a sucker. So she believed her husband and repeated, while looking around: "This is our lucky day, this is our lucky day."

The basket of the woman was full of fish by now. When she and her husband reached the banks the farmer ran ahead of her, looked into the thicket and said:

"Yesterday I laid out my nets and I want to check whether I've caught any fish or shrimps." A few minutes later the wife heard the husband shout:

"Run and see what I've caught! What extraordinary luck! I've fished a rabbit!" They were walking back home and the wife kept talking excitedly about the great dinner with the doughnuts, the fish and the rabbit. The husband said: "Let's go by the wood again. We could find other doughnuts!"

They went to the spot where the farmer had hidden his gold coins. The farmer pretended to find something.

"Look over here! There's a strange bag and . . . it's full of gold! This is an enchanted forest. We found the doughnuts on the trees, then we found the trout in the grass and now . . . gold." The poor woman was so excited that tears filled her eyes. She could not utter another word and gulped as she touched the shiny coins.

At home, after dinner, neither of the two could fall asleep. The farmer and his wife kept getting up to look over the treasure they had hidden in an old boot. The day after the farmer went back to work, but first said to his wife:

"Don't tell anybody about what happened yesterday." And he repeated the same recommendation every day after that. Pretty soon, however, the entire village had heard about the treasure. The farmer and his wife were called by the baron and when they went in to see him the farmer tried to stand behind his wife. His

wife, at the request of the baron, spoke first of the doughnuts, then of the trout on the grass and lastly of the rabbit in the river. Meanwhile, behind her, the husband kept tapping his forehead with his finger and gesticulating to the baron. The baron began looking at the woman with pity.

"And then I bet you found a treasure, too."

"That's right, Sir!" the woman said. The baron turned to the farmer and, tapping his finger on his forehead sympathetically said:

"I see what you mean. Unfortunately, I have the same problem with my wife . . ."

The farmers were sent home and no one believed their story. And so the shrewd farmer didn't go to jail and spent his money wisely.

JACK AND THE BEANSTALK

Once upon a time there was a poor widow who lived with her son Jack in a little house. Their wealth consisted solely of a milking cow. When the cow had grown too old, the mother sent Jack to sell it. On his way to the market, the boy met a stranger.

"I will give you five magic beans for your cow," the stranger offered. Jack was unsure and hesitated for a while but then, enticed by the idea of such an extraordinary deal, he decided to accept. When he returned home, his mother was furious and reprimanded him sternly:

"You fool! What have you done? We needed the money to buy a calf. Now we don't have anything and we are even poorer." Jack felt guilty and sad.

"Only a fool would exchange a cow for five beans," his mother fumed.

Then, at the height of her exasperation, she threw the five beans out

of the window and sent Jack to bed with no dinner.

The morning after, when he stepped outside, Jack saw an amazing sight. A gigantic beanstalk, reaching far into the clouds, had grown overnight.

"The beans must have really been magic," Jack thought happily. Being very curious, the boy climbed the plant and once he reached the top of the stalk he found himself over the clouds.

While looking around in amazement, Jack saw a huge castle of grey stone.

"I wonder who lives there," he thought. Jack was very surprised to see a path leading to the castle. He cautiously stepped on the clouds and, when he saw that they held him up, he walked to the castle. As he stood in front of the huge gate, his curiosity increased. He knocked several times on the gigantic door, but no one came to open it. Jack noticed that the door wasn't locked. With great effort, he was able to push it until it creaked open.

"What are you doing here?" a thundering voice asked. The biggest woman he had ever seen was scowling at him. Jack could only mutter:

"I am lost. May I have something to eat? I am very hungry." The woman, who did not have children, looked at him a little more kindly: "Come in, quick. I will give you a bowl of milk. But be careful because my husband, the ogre, eats children. If you hear him coming, hide at once."

Jack was shaking with fear but, nonetheless, he went inside. The milk the woman gave him was very good and Jack had almost finished drinking it when they heard a tremendous noise. The ogre was home.

"Fee fi fo fum! I smell the blood of an Englishman!" the ogre shouted.

"Hide, quick!" the woman whispered, pushing Jack into the oven.

"Do I smell a child in this room?" the ogre asked suspiciously, sniffing and looking all around.

"A child?" the woman repeated. "You see and hear children everywhere. That's all you ever think about. Sit down and I'll make your dinner." The ogre, still grumbling, filled a jug of wine and drank it all with his dinner.

After having counted again and again all the gold pieces of his treasure, the ogre fell asleep with his feet propped up on the table. After a little while, his thundering snoring echoed throughout the castle. The ogre's wife went to prepare the ogre's bed and Jack, who had sneaked out of the oven, saw the gold pieces on the table and filled a little bag full of them.

"I hope he won't see me, otherwise he'll eat me whole," Jack thought while shivering with fear. Jack's heart was beating faster, not just faster because he feared the ogre but because he was very excited. Thanks to all the gold coins, he and his mother would be rich. Jack ran down the path over the clouds.

Jack arrived at the top of the giant beanstalk and began to descend as quickly as possible, hanging on to the leaves and the branches. When he finally reached the ground, he found his mother waiting for him. The poor woman had been worried sick since his disappearance.

She had been frightened by the giant beanstalk. When she saw Jack come down and then triumphantly hold up the bag full of gold, she burst out crying.

"Where have you been, my son? Do you want me to die worrying? What kind of plant is this? What . . ." Jack cheerfully interrupted her, emptying the contents of the bag before her.

"You see, I did the right thing exchanging that cow for the magic beans. Now I'll tell you the whole story . . ."

And Jack told his mother everything that had happened in detail. In the days that followed, the widow's humble house was made into a comfortable home. The gold pieces were spent to buy a lot of things Jack and his mother never had before. Mother and son were very happy. But as time went by, so did the money. When the last gold piece had been spent, Jack decided to go back to the castle above the clouds. This time the boy went inside through the kitchen and hid once again in the oven. Shortly after, the ogre came in and began to sniff about.

"I smell children," he said to his wife. But since she had seen no one come in, she didn't pay any attention to him.

After dinner, the ogre placed a hen on the table. The hen laid golden eggs. Jack saw the miraculous hen from a crack in the oven door. He waited for the ogre to fall asleep, jumped out of the oven, snatched the hen and ran out of the castle. The hen's squawking, however, woke up the ogre.

"Thief! Thief!" he shouted. But Jack was already far away. Once again, he found his mother anxiously waiting for him at the foot of the beanstalk.

"Is that all you stole? A hen?" she asked Jack, disappointed. But Jack ran, happy, to the court yard.

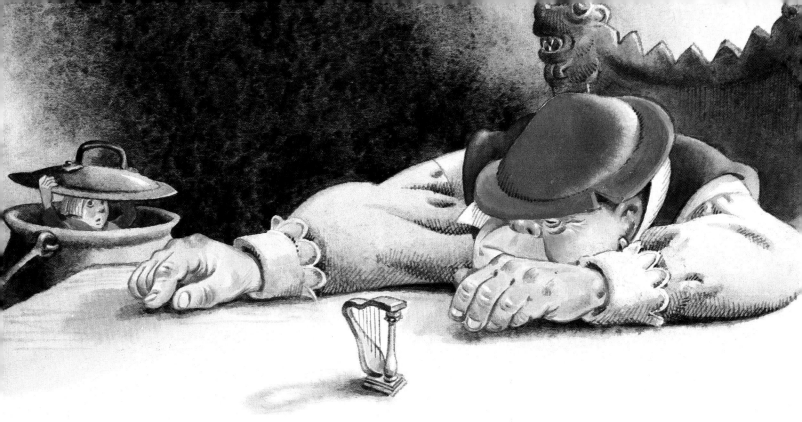

"Just wait," he said to his mother. As a matter of fact, a little while later the hen laid a golden egg and continued to lay such an egg every single day after that.

By now, Jack and his mother were very wealthy. Their house was completely rebuilt. Teams of carpenters replaced the roof, added new rooms and elegant marble columns. Then they bought paintings, tapestries, Persian rugs, mirrors and many other beautiful furnishings. Their miserable shack was transformed into a luxurious home.

Jack and his mother had not forgotten their previous years of poverty and deprivation. So they chose to welcome any traveller who needed food or shelter. But wealth doesn't always bring happiness. Jack's mother suddenly fell ill or so it seemed. But not one of the many doctors who visited her could discover what her illness was. The woman was sad, ate less and less and showed no interest in life. She rarely smiled, and then only when Jack was near to her. Her son tried to cheer her up, but nothing could save the mother from her slow but inevitable decline. Even a circus's famous clown, who had been invited especially for her entertainment, received only a sad greeting.

Jack was desperate and didn't know what to do. All the hen's gold was not enough to make his mother well again. So he had another idea.

"What if I went back to the ogre's castle? Maybe there I could find the answer," he thought. He shivered with fear thinking about the giant's huge hands and mouth, but the hope of helping his mother encouraged him to face the danger again. One evening he gathered all his courage and climbed once more the giant beanstalk. This time he entered the castle through an open window. He sneaked in the darkness to the kitchen and hid inside a huge pot until the following day. After dinner the ogre went to get his magic harp, an instrument that sang and played marvellous music. While listening to the harp's sweet melody, the ogre fell asleep. In his hiding place, Jack was captivated by the harp's song as well. When he finally heard the ogre snore loudly, he lifted the pot's lid and saw the extraordinary instrument: a golden harp.

He quickly climbed on the table and ran away with the harp in his hands. The instrument woke up the ogre screaming:

"Master, master! Wake up! A thief is taking me away!" The ogre woke up suddenly, was disorientated for a couple of seconds but then realized what was happening and began chasing Jack. The boy ran as fast as he could and the harp kept calling out.

"Shut up! Shut up! If you'll play for me, you'll be happier," Jack kept telling it breathlessly. He finally arrived to where the leafy top of the beanstalk poked through the clouds. Jack crept along the ground and slipped down the stalk quietly. The harp did not make a sound and the ogre didn't see Jack go down the plant. When Jack got down to earth he called to his mother,

"Look what I've brought you!" The harp began to play an enchanting melody and his mother smiled happily.

But up there in the clouds someone else had heard the harp's beautiful song and Jack soon realized with terror that the thick beanstalk was shaking under a very heavy weight. The ogre was coming down to earth!

"Hide the harp and bring me an axe! I must chop down the plant before the ogre gets here," Jack said to his mother. They could already see the ogre's huge boots when the plant and the ogre finally crashed to the ground. The ogre fell down a cliff nearby. The ogre's wife never found out what had happened to her husband and as time passed Jack no longer felt in danger.

The magical sound of the harp cured his mother's sadness and she was once again happy and cheerful. The hen kept on laying golden eggs. Jack's life had gone through a lot of changes since he had accepted the magic beans. But without his courage and his wit, he and his mother could never have found happiness.

THE EMPEROR'S NEW CLOTHES

Once upon a time there lived a vain emperor whose only worry in life was to dress in elegant clothes. He changed clothes almost every hour and loved to show them off to his people.

Word of the Emperor's refined habits spread over his kingdom and beyond. Two scoundrels who had heard of the Emperor's vanity decided to take advantage of it. They introduced themselves at the gates of the palace with a scheme in mind.

"We are two very good tailors and after many years of research we have invented an extraordinary method to weave a cloth so light and fine that it looks invisible. As a matter of fact it is invisible to anyone who is too stupid and incompetent to appreciate its quality."

The chief of the guards heard the scoundrel's strange story and sent for the court chamberlain. The chamberlain notified the prime minister, who ran to the Emperor and disclosed the incredible news. The Emperor's curiosity got the better of him and he decided to see the two scoundrels.

"Besides being invisible, your Highness, this cloth will be woven in colours and patterns created especially for you." The emperor gave the two men a bag of gold coins in exchange for their promise to begin working on the fabric immediately.

"Just tell us what you need to get started and we'll give it to you." The two scoundrels asked for a loom,

35

silk, gold thread and then pretended to begin working. The Emperor thought he had spent his money quite well: in addition to getting a new extraordinary suit, he would discover which of his subjects were ignorant and incompetent. A few days later, he called the old and wise prime minister, who was considered by everyone as a man with common sense.

"Go and see how the work is proceeding," the Emperor told him, "and come back to let me know."

The prime minister was welcomed by the two scoundrels.

"We're almost finished, but we need a lot more gold thread. Here, Excellency! Admire the colours, feel the softness!" The old man bent over the loom and tried to see the fabric that was not there. He felt cold sweat on his forehead.

"I can't see anything," he thought. "If I see nothing, that means I'm stupid! Or, worse, incompetent!" If the prime minister admitted that he didn't see anything, he would be discharged from his office.

"What a marvellous fabric," he said then. "I'll certainly tell the Emperor." The two scoundrels rubbed their hands gleefully. They had almost made it. More thread was requested to finish the work.

Finally, the Emperor received the announcement that the two tailors had come to take all the measurements needed to sew his new suit.

"Come in," the Emperor ordered. Even as they bowed, the two scoundrels pretended to be holding a large roll of fabric.

"Here it is, your Highness, the result of our labour," the scoundrels said. "We have worked night and day but, at last, the most beautiful fabric in the world is ready for you. Look at the colours and feel how fine it is." Of course the Emperor did not see any colours and could not feel any cloth between his fingers. He panicked and felt like fainting. But luckily the throne was right behind him and he sat down. But when he realized that no one could know that he did not see the fabric, he felt better. Nobody could find out he was stupid and incompetent. And the Emperor didn't know that everybody else around him thought and did the very same thing.

The farce continued as the two scoundrels had foreseen it. Once they had taken the measurements, the two began cutting the air with scissors while sewing with their needles an invisible cloth.

"Your Highness, you'll have to take off your clothes to try on your new ones." The two scoundrels draped the new clothes on him and then held up a mirror. The Emperor was embarrassed but since none of his bystanders were, he felt relieved.

"Yes, this is a beautiful suit and it looks very good on me," the Emperor said trying to look comfortable. "You've done a fine job."

"Your Majesty," the prime minister said, "we have a request for you. The people have found out about this extraordinary fabric and they are anxious to see you in your new suit." The Emperor was doubtful about showing himself naked to the people, but then he abandoned his fears. After all, no one would know about it except the ignorant and the incompetent!

"All right," he said. "I will grant the people this privilege." He summoned his carriage and the ceremonial parade was formed. A group of dignitaries walked at the very front of the procession and anxiously scrutinized the faces of the people in the street. All the people had gathered in the main square, pushing and shoving to get a better look. An applause welcomed the regal procession. Everyone wanted to know how stupid or incompetent his or her neighbour was but, as the Emperor passed, a strange murmur rose from the crowd.

Everyone said, loud enough for the others to hear:

"Look at the Emperor's new clothes. They're beautiful!"

"What a marvellous train!"

"And the colours! The colours of that beautiful fabric! I have never seen anything like it in my life." They all tried to conceal their disappointment at not being able to see the clothes, and since nobody was willing to admit his own stupidity and incompetence, they all behaved as the two scoundrels had predicted.

A child, however, who had no important job and could only see things as his eyes showed them to him, went up to the carriage.

"The Emperor is naked," he said.

"Fool!" his father reprimanded, running after him. "Don't talk nonsense!" He grabbed his child and took him away. But the boy's remark, which had been heard by the bystanders, was repeated over and over again until everyone cried:

"The boy is right! The Emperor is naked! It's true!"

The Emperor realized that the people were right but could not admit to that. He though it better to continue the procession under the illusion that anyone who couldn't see his clothes was either stupid or incompetent. And he stood stiffly on his carriage, while behind him a page held his imaginary mantle.

SIX ABLE MEN

Once upon a time there lived a young soldier named Martin who had enlisted in the royal army to fight a war. The war was long but victorious and when the King abandoned the enemy's territory and returned with his troops to the homeland, he left Martin to guard the only bridge on the river that separated the two nations.

"Stay on watch on the bridge," the King ordered. "Don't let any enemy soldier go by." Days and then months passed, and the soldier kept his watch on the bridge. He survived by asking the passers-by for food and, after two years, thought that the authorities had probably forgotten him. He then headed towards the capital, where he would ask the King for all his back pay. His pockets were empty and his only possessions were a pipe, a bit of tobacco and his sword.

A couple of days later he arrived in a valley where a stream crossed his path. A big man with hands as big as hams, large shoulders and a bull's neck was sitting by the stream. The man, who had a strangely soft and kind voice, asked him:

"Would you like to cross the stream?" The soldier couldn't ask for more. The man effortlessly uprooted a huge tree and laid it across the stream. Martin offered the man some of his tobacco in return and when he found out that the man had nothing to do, Martin asked him to come along.

"You'll see all the things we can do together!"

They had just begun walking away when they met a hunter who was aiming his rifle at a faraway hill.

"What are you aiming at?"

"Do you see that cobweb on that tree on top of the hill?" the hunter asked. "I want to get the spider!" The hunter shot and

when the three men got to the top of the hill they found a big hole in the middle of the cobweb and no more spider. Martin had never seen anyone shoot that well and he asked the hunter to join them.

"Come with us and you'll be in luck!" The three men walked and walked until they arrived at a windmill. The wheel of the mill was turning even though there was no wind. The men were puzzled but further up the road they found a fat man sitting on a tree stump. The man was blowing through one of his nostrils in the mill's direction. The fat man explained to the three amazed fellow travellers that his strength was such that he could sneeze

up a hurricane. The soldier convinced him to follow them. As they approached the city, they were approached by a man who hopped about with his legs tied together.

"Who tied you up?" they asked in unison.

"I did it myself," the man, who was very young and very thin, answered. "If I untied myself I would run as fast as the wind and would not enjoy the sights." And so it was that even this character, nicknamed Fastfoot by the others, joined the group.

But the surprises of that extraordinary day were far from over. A little man with a round face sat under a tree. He held his hat over his left ear. "If I straighten my hat," he explained, "I will freeze everything around me." Naturally, everybody took his word for it and the stranger was asked to join the group. The bizarre company finally arrived at the city. A public notice was hung outside the city walls. The princess announced that whoever would beat her in a race could marry her.

The soldier dusted his uniform, cleaned himself up after the long trip and ran to the palace. He wanted to challenge the princess but said that one of his servants would run in his place. The princess accepted his challenge. The morning after, at the starting line, Fastfoot untied his legs and took off like a rocket. Each one of the contestants had a jug that had to be filled at a nearby stream and brought back full to the finish line. On his way back, Fastfoot stopped to pick a flower and after carefully setting the jug on the ground and realizing that the princess was still far away, he decided to lie down and rest for a while. Unfortunately, he fell asleep.

Later on, when the princess caught up with him and saw that he had fallen asleep, she kicked down his jug and ran away. She was sure of her victory. From far away the sharp sighted hunter shot and hit a spot near Fastfoot's ear. Fastfoot woke up all of a sudden and saw the princess approaching the finish line. He quickly ran back to the stream, filled the jug and reached the finish line as fast as lightning. The King was furious. He would never let his daughter marry a miserable soldier.

He invited the unsuspecting Martin to the palace. Martin told him about his two years watching over the river, which made the King ever angrier. The King, however, pretended to feel guilty and invited the soldier and his friends to a banquet in a strange dining room. In fact the dining room was lined with iron walls and was built over a huge furnace. The King ordered his men to seal the dining room's door and to light the furnace. Then he proceeded to watch the slow death of the group through an unbreakable glass. The six men began eating but suddenly felt the floor grow very hot, while the room's temperature rapidly increased.

But Martin did not lose his head. He straightened the hat of the round faced little man and pretty soon they were all shivering from the cold. The King uselessly urged his men to throw more and more wood in the furnace, but the soldier and his friends had found a remedy to the King's wickedness. No one had ever come out of this torture chamber alive, but this time the King had to accept defeat, even though he was still determined not to let his daughter go. He offered the soldier a large sum of money as long as he gave up the wedding.

"I will fill you a bag of gold and other riches if you forget the wedding."

"That's fine with me," Martin said, "and I accept your offer but as long as I pick the bag and the man who will carry it away." The poor King was unaware of the strength of one of the six friends. When he began filling the sack, all of his gold was not enough to fill it. Martin and his friends were rich. When they left court, the King had become very poor.

The monarch lost his temper and realized the soldier had fooled him. He called the army commander and ordered two battalions to chase Martin. "Bring them back dead or alive and at all costs!" Later on, the soldiers caught up with the six young men and surrounded them.

"Give us back the gold and surrender," they demanded. But the fattest of the men began blowing so hard that horses and soldiers were carried away. In just a few minutes the wounded soldiers were scattered all over the plain and the battalions were no longer a threat to the six extraordinary friends who continued their journey.

Then they divided the gold and jewels in equal parts and each one of them went his own separate way. Martin crossed the bridge where he had been on watch for so long without any reward and never turned back again.

THE SEVEN CROWS

Once upon a time there was, far away amid high mountains, a green valley. The valley was crossed by a clear stream and a woodsman had built his stone house on its shore.

The woodsman was married and had seven sons and one daughter. He often had to travel from home to work and his wife had a hard time bringing up the children alone. The daughter did not cause her any trouble because she was kind, pretty and helpful. But the boys were the cause of her problems because they were rude, disobedient and quarrelsome. They had no respect for their mother and she was very worried for them.

When the husband returned home tired after a week's hard work, the poor wife couldn't bring herself to tell him of the sons' mischievous behaviour because she didn't want to worry him further. The woman kept her sorrow to herself not realizing that by doing so her sons would only get worse and worse. As a matter of fact, when their father was not home to punish them, the boys kept on taking advantage of the situation which continued to get worse.

Their sister suffered most because she loved her brothers even if they were wicked, but she loved her mother especially. Being the youngest, however, none of the brothers paid any attention to her reprimands.

One day the seven boys got into the biggest trouble yet. In the woods grew a dangerous grass which causes the animals stomachs to swell. The woodsman had always told his sons to make sure that their goats never ate any. The cruel boys filled a bag with the grass and then mixed it in with the animals' food. Later on the goats and the cow fell ill, their bellies swelled and ached and they could not stand up.

"We won't have any more milk! We won't be able to make any cheese!" the mother cried desperately. "How will we survive?" The sons laughed maliciously and did not realize the evil they had done until the woman, at the height of her desperation, cried:

"I wish you were crows rather than sons of mine!" When she spoke these words, a mysterious cloud overshadowed the sun, it was suddenly very chilly and the boys turned into seven big crows that flew away croaking.

The woman was so frightened and felt such regret that she fainted. When the father came back from work the day after, he found out the truth and was very upset. Nevertheless he tried to comfort his wife, telling her she was not to blame for the terrible wish that had been fulfilled. But the house was filled with sadness and despair.

A long time passed and the little girl grew older. She still remembered her brothers and rarely smiled. One day she asked her mother's permission to go and look for them.

"I will find them, I feel it. I feel I have to go and that they are expecting me. Let me go, Mother, and give me your blessing." The mother could not resist her daughter's pleas and the little girl left home with a little bundle of provisions. She walked for two days through the woods, climbing towards the mountains. Pretty soon she had no more food, her clothes were torn and she was cold and tired.

The third day, at dawn, she saw a strange little cottage in the mist. Something attracted her to the house even though it had a gloomy and uninviting appearance. When she was inside the house she found a little table with seven bowls on it and her heart beat very fast . . . maybe she had found what she was looking for. There was a large pot full of wheat and oats on the fire.

The little girl was very hungry and so she poured a bit of food in a bowl and ate it avidly. Then she went upstairs and found a little bedroom with seven little beds, each one with a different blanket. With tears in her eyes, the little girl realized she had finally found her brothers. Exhausted by the trip and the commotion, the little girl lay down on a bed and fell asleep.

Later on, seven chattering crows pushed open the front door and sat around the kitchen table.

"Someone has eaten some of our soup," one of the crows said after finding the dirty bowl.

"But who would ever come up here?" answered another.

"We're condemned to be alone on these mountains forever."

"Nobody will ever come to look for us." When they finished eating, the crows pulled on their sleeping caps, went upstairs and found the little girl in one of their beds.

"But this is . . ." one of the crows said, after delicately touching her braid with his beak.

"That's right, this is . . . our sister," they said all together. At that moment the little girl opened her eyes and when she saw herself surrounded by the big and ugly birds, she was frightened. But out of one ugly beak spoke a kind voice:

"Are you our sister?" The little girl got up and opened her arms:

"I've found you! I've found you! We're together again at last!" The seven crows looked at her sadly and one said:

"Don't we frighten and disgust you?" The girl hugged every one of them.

"I love you very much and even if you've turned into crows you're still my brothers." When they heard this, the crows were moved and began crying.

"Why don't you come back home with me?" she asked.

"We would like very much to come back," they all answered together, "and we regret our evil ways. But how can we show ourselves to our parents like this?"

"Mother would accept you all the same, I am sure of it. She keeps crying and thinking of you," the little girl answered.

The little girl insisted and convinced her brothers to come home with her.

"There's no need to walk back up and down the mountains like you did. We will fly there and carry you," they said. As they were about to leave, the youngest brother said,

"Wait a minute! Let's bring Mother all the sparkling stones we found as a present."

"They are really beautiful," the little girl said when she saw the bag with her brothers' treasure.

"Do you like them? They might be precious, you know. When we crows see something sparkle, we cannot help ourselves and take it."

"This one sparkles more than the rest, maybe it's a diamond." They finally left. The world was very different from above. At first the little girl was scared, but the seven crows held her firmly and flew safely. Then they saw the valley, the stream and the little house where they were born. The courtyard was deserted and when they landed the little girl said,

"You wait here and I'll go and call Mother."

She silently went into the kitchen and saw the poor woman leaning on the table and weeping. She hugged her and kissed her saying,

"Mother I'm back and I have a big surprise for you."

"You're here at last! I thought I'd lost you forever." The poor woman was so happy and moved that she didn't know whether to laugh or to cry. In the courtyard she found the crows.

"My poor sons! I missed you so much. I am so sorry to have uttered that curse. A mother should never say such things against her children."

"We regret all we have done too. We very much regret our wickedness." They were all crying over the past when, suddenly, another miracle occurred. The seven brothers became boys again. The father, who had heard voices, ran out of the house.

"Thank God I can see my children again," he cried as he hugged his sons and his daughter.

The years passed and the crows' hats became the only memory of this moving story.

The stones the crows had brought to their mother turned out to be precious after all, and the treasure allowed the family to live a better future.